NO DOGS HERE!

· KATHRYN HEWITT ·

Dutton Children's Books · New York

DUTTON CHILDREN'S BOOKS
A division of Penguin Young Readers Group
Published by the Penguin Group
Penguin Group (USA) Inc., 375 Hudson Street, New York, New York 10014, U.S.A.
Penguin Group (Canada), 10 Alcorn Avenue, Toronto, Ontario, Canada M4V 3B2
(a division of Pearson Penguin Canada Inc.)
Penguin Books Ltd, 80 Strand, London WC2R 0RL, England
Penguin Ireland, 25 St Stephen's Green, Dublin 2, Ireland
(a division of Penguin Books Ltd)
Penguin Group (Australia), 250 Camberwell Road, Camberwell, Victoria 3124, Australia
(a division of Pearson Australia Group Pty Ltd)
Penguin Books India Pvt Ltd, 11 Community Centre, Panchsheel Park, New Delhi–110 017, India
Penguin Group (NZ), Cnr Airborne and Rosedale Roads, Albany, Auckland 1310, New Zealand
(a division of Pearson New Zealand Ltd)
Penguin Books (South Africa) (Pty) Ltd, 24 Sturdee Avenue, Rosebank, Johannesburg 2196, South Africa
Penguin Books Ltd, Registered Offices: 80 Strand, London WC2R 0RL, England

LIBRARY OF CONGRESS CATALOGING-IN-PUBLICATION DATA
Hewitt, Kathryn.
No dogs here!/by Kathryn Hewitt.—1st ed.
p. cm.
Summary: Upon realizing that lack of clothing is the only thing keeping dogs out of many places,
Norman, Ginger, and Rufus borrow clothes from their owners and have a wonderful time doing all the
things humans do, until they make a simple mistake.
ISBN 0-525-47200-2
[1. Dogs—Fiction. 2. Human-animal relationships—Fiction. 3. Clothing and dress—Fiction.
4. Humorous stories.] I. Title.
PZ7.H4493No 2005
[E]—dc22 2004021084

Published in the United States by Dutton Children's Books,
a division of Penguin Young Readers Group
345 Hudson Street, New York, New York 10014
www.penguin.com/youngreaders

Designed by Tim Hall and Jason Henry
Manufactured in China · First Edition
1 3 5 7 9 10 8 6 4 2

Every time Norman went walking with his owner, it was always the same.

"No Dogs Allowed" at the deli.

"No Dogs Here" at the park.

"No Dogs Allowed" at the beauty parlor.

"No Dogs Here" at the ice-cream shop.

NO DOGS
HERE

101
Flavors

"It's not fair," Norman said to his friends Ginger and Rufus. "People have all the fun. What makes them better than us?"

"They don't have fleas?" Rufus guessed.

"Nah, it's the clothes," said Ginger.

"Of course!" said Norman.

On Monday, after their owners went to work, Norman,
Ginger, and Rufus borrowed some of their things.

They met in front of the library.
"Do you think we'll pass as people?" asked Rufus.
"No Dogs Here!" said Ginger.
"Well then, I suggest we go inside," Norman said.

They spent the day lolling around the reading room,
wallowing in books. No one gave them any trouble. Norman
even checked out some books with his owner's card.

"I think I like books better than bones," said Rufus.
"Yes, there's nothing quite as satisfying as a good read," said Norman.

"Shall we try a more daring adventure tomorrow?" asked Ginger.

"Perhaps," said Norman. "But let's go home and change before our owners get back."

On Tuesday they went to Poochini's for lunch and shared a deep-dish mega meat pizza.

"Should we ask for a doggie bag?" Rufus chuckled.

They went wild at the pet store on Wednesday.
"We know some DOGS that will just love this stuff,"
said Ginger.

On Thursday they spun their wheels at the skateboard park.

"Dogabunga, dude!" cried Rufus.

No bikes
No gum
No dogs

Friday was hotter than a parked car with the windows rolled up.

"I wish we could go someplace wet," whined Ginger.

"And do the doggie paddle," added Rufus.

"I suppose we could . . ." said Norman.

They put on swimsuits and calmly strolled to the pool.
But when they saw the water, they couldn't resist shedding
some clothes.

"Hot dog!" they all yelped as they jumped into the pool.

The manager called their owners. "I know just the place to straighten out these naughty, soggy dogs," she told them.

Norman, Ginger, and Rufus spent the next six weeks at Miss Behave's Obedience School.

At graduation, their owners were very proud.

"He can sit!"

"He can shake!"

"She can roll over!"

The three dogs had learned an important lesson . . .

Leave your dog tags
at home when you go
out on the town.